BETTY REN WRIGHT

Christina's
Ghost

HOLIDAY HOUSE / NEW YORK

Library of Congress Cataloging-in-Publication Data

Wright, Betty Ren.
  Christina's ghost.

  SUMMARY; Christina's summer in a spooky, isolated
Victorian house with her grumpy uncle turns into a ghostly
adventure.
  1. Children's stories, American. [1. Ghosts—
Fiction. 2. Mystery and detective stories] I. Title.
PZ7.W933Ch 1985 [Fic]   85-42880
ISBN   0-8234-0581-8

ISBN-13: 978-0-8234-0581-7 (hardcover)
ISBN-13: 978-0-8234-2171-8 (paperback)

Contents

1.

"Tears Won't Help!"

"Chrissy's going to throw up again!" Jenny shrieked the news.

The back of Uncle Ralph's thin neck turned red. He swung the car off the road and braked at the edge of a steep slope. Chris hurtled out of the car. Halfway down the hill, she knelt and waited for the waves of sickness to overwhelm her.

Nothing happened. A breeze cooled her forehead. The air was sweet after the pizza-and-oranges smell of Uncle Ralph's old Chevy. At the bottom of the hill, a stream glittered in the sun.

Neat, Chris thought. She wished she could stay right there. She wished she could walk to Grandma's house in Oakleigh. Or fly! She was sure that if she got back in the car, she'd be sick again.

"How about it, Christina? We haven't got forever."

Chris looked up and saw Uncle Ralph and Jenny peering down at her. Uncle Ralph sounded annoyed, as usual. He sometimes called Jenny "old girl," and he called other people "sport" or "Buster." But he always called Christina Christina.

"You look sort of green," Jenny said when they were back in the car. "Sort of green and sort of gray. Very yucky."

"That's how I feel," Chris told her. "Open the window on your side, okay? And don't eat any more oranges."

For the next hour Chris kept her face turned to the open window and tried to think good thoughts. Going to Grandma's was okay to think about. If she had to be away from home, she'd rather be out in the country with Grandma than anywhere else. Thinking about home, even for a second, was a mistake. Every time she pictured her house standing empty, she began to feel sick again. By now her parents were in Seattle, on their way to five weeks of conference-and-vacation in Alaska. *No, don't think about that.*

Think about sleeping in a sleeping bag out under the trees. Grandma let her do that, as often as she wanted. Think about fishing in the little river a quarter-mile away. Think about exploring the old barn, or climbing to the very top of the oak in Grandma's front yard. Last summer she'd scrambled two-thirds of the way to the top before Jenny saw her and tattled.

The wind blew Uncle Ralph's visored cap from the back-window shelf onto Chris's lap. She slicked her dark hair behind her ears and put on the cap, tilting it to one side. Then she leaned over the seat and twisted the rear-view mirror so she could see herself.

"Will you cut that out?" Uncle Ralph pushed the mirror back into position. His long, narrow face glowered at her. "And take off my hat. If you please."

Jenny giggled. Chris took off the hat.

"You don't like me," she said softly, but of course Uncle Ralph heard.

"I do like you," he said. "It's just that you always get things in a muddle, Christina. You don't think. I'm a past-middle-aged man, and I suppose I have past-middle-aged opinions. I happen to believe a girl should . . . should act like a lady. And dress like one," he added.

Chris considered throwing the cap at him and decided she'd better not. She glanced down at herself and then at Jenny. Her sister's jeans looked brand-new; Chris's were worn almost to whiteness, the way she liked them. Jenny wore a crisp red-and-white plaid

shirt, and Chris wore a T-shirt with a Spider-Man
picture on the front and a hole under one arm. Even
though Jenny was only eight, two years younger than
Chris, she insisted on blow-drying her pale brown hair
so that it fell in waves around her face. Chris didn't
care how her own hair looked, as long as it didn't get
in her way.

"Chrissy is a tomboy," Jenny commented. "She can't
help the way she is."

Chris threw the cap at her.

"Can we just forget it?" Uncle Ralph said. "Tomboys
are okay. You're fine, Christina."

But Chris knew he was counting the minutes until
he could drop her, and Jenny, too, at Grandma's house.
Her mother had said they were lucky Uncle Ralph had
even consented to take them with him on his way north.
He was an associate professor at City College, and
every summer he went off somewhere by himself. This
year a friend had asked him to house-sit at a northern
Wisconsin lake. Chris's mother said the human race
was just too much for her brother Ralph. He liked his
own company best.

"Chrissy bites her fingernails," Jenny said. "I wish
she wouldn't. It makes me sick."

"And I wish I was an only child," Chris snapped.

Uncle Ralph switched on a classical music station

and turned up the volume. He looked straight ahead, as if he were pretending he was alone in the car.

When they turned down the gravel lane that led to Grandma's house, Chris looked around eagerly. There was the big gray house. The old sheepdog, Maggie, lay under the oak tree. There was the barn, its door open and inviting. There was the porch swing, and the red wagon planted full of white petunias. Everything looked exactly as it had a year ago when they'd come with their parents, and the year before that. Grandma never went racing off to Alaska to a stupid conference. Grandma *loved* the human race. Suddenly, Chris couldn't wait to give her a hug.

"That's not Grandma," Jenny said. She pointed at the front door. The screen was partway open, and someone stood in the shadows. As the car turned into the yard, Aunt Grace, their mother's older sister, came out and waited at the top step.

"Oh, give me strength," Uncle Ralph muttered. "She has that look on her face."

"What look?" Jenny asked.

"Her the-world-would-be-a-mess-if-I-didn't-take-charge look," Uncle Ralph said. "That woman was born to give orders."

They climbed out of the car, and Chris took a big breath of country air. Aunt Grace marched down the steps, and Maggie the dog waddled toward them.

"I thought you'd never get here," Aunt Grace said, not bothering with hellos. "Whatever took you so long?"

Uncle Ralph scowled. "Christina had to make a few roadside stops," he said. "Where's Ma?"

"She's in the hospital, that's where." For just a second Aunt Grace's thin face sagged. Then she sniffed hard and went on. "Got taken with a gallbladder attack at five-thirty this morning. The Blackwells took her to the clinic in Rochester. Mrs. Blackwell just called— Ma's had her surgery, and she's doing fine."

Uncle Ralph sat down on a porch step with a thump. "Poor Ma," he said. "Why didn't you go with her?"

"No need," Aunt Grace retorted. "And she said to tell you not to go dashing over there till she feels better." She rolled her eyes at Chris and Jenny. "We've got our problems right here."

Uncle Ralph narrowed his eyes. He looked at the girls as if he'd never seen them before. "What do you mean *we?*" he demanded. "You're here. You can look after them till Ma gets back."

Aunt Grace gave an angry squeak. "I'm not *staying* here, Ralph Cummings," she said. "I just drove out from town to tell you the news and close things up. The Blackwells will stop by every day to take care of Maggie. I have a house of my own to look after in Titusville. And three cats. No one can expect me to take over a family of children just because their parents want to go gallivanting off to Alaska."

Chris felt her face burn, but she was too scared to say anything. Out of the corner of her eye, she saw Jenny shrink back.

"Then you can take the kids to town with you," Uncle Ralph said, getting up from the step. "I'm on my way."

Aunt Grace moved between him and the car. "I have it all figured out, Ralph," she said. "I have only one bedroom, but it has twin beds. Jennifer can stay with me, and you'll take Christina. We can't reach Jean and Philip today, but I'll call their hotel in Anchorage and leave a message about what's happened."

"I'll take Christina?" Uncle Ralph looked at Aunt Grace as if he couldn't believe what he'd heard. "Me? Christina can sleep on your couch."

"It's a loveseat. Too short."

"She has a sleeping bag with her. She can sleep on the floor."

"No!" Two bright red spots flamed on Aunt Grace's cheeks. Her glasses flashed in the sun. "I can't cope with *two* children," she said. "I can't and I won't. You have to do your part in this emergency, Ralph. Don't you dare turn your back on your family in its hour of need."

Jenny started to cry, even though she was the one

who was wanted.

"Nobody has to take me," Chris said. "I'll stay here with Maggie until Grandma comes home."

Aunt Grace looked disgusted. "Don't be silly. You and Uncle Ralph will have a good time together. You can get to know each other real well."

"He doesn't want to get to know me," Chris said. "And I don't want to get to know him." To her horror, she began to cry, too.

"Chrissy's crying," Jenny marveled through her own tears. "I never saw her cry before. Not ever."

The grownups stared. "Tears won't help," Aunt Grace said finally. "No need to get upset, Christina." She glared at Uncle Ralph. "You've made the poor girl feel unwanted," she said. "Poor child."

Uncle Ralph looked as if he had a mouthful of vinegar. He opened the car trunk and tossed out Jenny's brown duffel bag.

"Anything else of yours here?" he asked fiercely.

Jenny shook her head.

"Then get in the car, Christina."

"No!"

"Get in, I said. Now! We have three hours of driving ahead of us."

Chris looked at Jenny, the chosen child. She looked at Grandma's empty house, and at Maggie, who seemed puzzled. Chris felt as if only Maggie understood her.

They were both in the way.

"Get *in,* Christina."

Chris got in the car. There was nothing else to do.

She wondered how many times she'd be sick in the next three hours.

2.

The Strange House in the Woods

"Ugh!"

Chris's eyes flew open. She sat up straight. Beside her, Uncle Ralph clutched the steering wheel and groaned with every bump.

"It's okay, baby," he muttered. Chris realized he was talking to his car. "Hang in there, sport."

They were on a narrow, winding road. Trees brushed the car windows, and the headlight beams bounced against a curtain of green.

"Are we nearly there?" Chris asked.

"We'd better be," Uncle Ralph snapped. His longish gray hair straggled across his forehead. Even his dark mustache looked flustered.

12

The Chevy made another jouncing turn and stopped. They were on a wide stretch of overgrown lawn.

"Well, well," Uncle Ralph said. "How about that?"

Chris stared. There was light here, beyond the tree-lined road. Before them was one of the strangest houses she'd ever seen. It had towers and gables, and carved trimmings over every window. The whole house was painted a sickly gray-green. It looked like a moldy wedding cake.

"I thought we were going to a *cottage*," Chris said, when she could speak. "Maybe a log cabin. On a lake."

"Well, there's certainly a lake," Uncle Ralph said. "Use your eyes, Christina."

Sure enough, metal-colored water glinted beyond the house.

"I never said it was a cottage," Uncle Ralph went on. "My friend inherited this place from his uncle. It was the old family home—people called Charles. Something happened—something pretty bad, I guess—and they moved out." He began lifting boxes and suitcases from the car. "The uncle looked after the house for the last thirty years—tried to sell it, but there weren't any takers. My friend's going to unload it this fall, as soon as he gets back from Europe."

Uncle Ralph turned to look at the house again. "He may just have to give it away," he said thoughtfully.

Chris realized that the house had taken him by surprise, too.

She picked up her suitcase and followed Uncle Ralph across the grass and up the steps. The key to the back door was very big. It turned with a scratchy sound, and they went inside. Uncle Ralph muttered to himself as he searched for a light switch.

Chris felt a moment of panic before the weak overhead light flicked on and showed them the huge, old-fashioned kitchen. The floor was made of bricks; there was a smell of musty pipes.

"Cozy as a tomb," Uncle Ralph said. Chris agreed with him. She stayed so close as he led the way through the downstairs that a couple of times she stepped on his heels.

"Christina, there's plenty of room in here. No need to walk on me."

"Sorry." *What a crab!* she thought. And there were days and days—maybe weeks—of crabbiness ahead!

She followed Uncle Ralph down the hall, past a tiny bathroom under the stairs, and into a wide foyer. On the left was a parlor crowded with furniture. On the right was a formal dining room. Even with the lights turned on, shadows filled every corner.

They crossed the dining room into a smaller room with a fireplace and a desk. Books lined two walls and part of a third. "This will do for my study," Uncle Ralph said, sounding a little less grumpy. He ran his fingers over a row of books. "You can go along upstairs and pick out a bedroom, Christina. Take your duffel bag with you, please."

Chris went back to the front hall and looked up the stairs to the darkness above. Suddenly the house seemed to close around her like a trap. She struggled with the front door until it opened, and stepped outside just as Uncle Ralph came into the hall.

"I bet this place is haunted," she challenged him through the screen.

Uncle Ralph shook his head. "A typical Christina comment," he said. "Don't be silly."

Chris fled across the wide porch and down the steps. A flagstone path led to the shore, ending at a pier built of concrete slabs. Her sneakers made a soft slap-slap sound as she darted to its very end. She threw herself down and pressed her face against the concrete. It was still warm from the setting sun.

For the second time that day, tears dampened her cheeks. "Who cares what *he* says?" she whispered to herself. "He's the silly one, not me."

After a while she lifted her head and looked down at the water licking the pilings. It made a good sound, like chuckling voices. Two ducks skittered across the surface of the lake, then settled peacefully in the water. On either side of the lawn, trees crowded down to the shore.

Chris took a quavery breath and sat up. The lake was beautiful. She was happy to have a lake, even if everything else was dreadful.

She swung around, aware that someone was watching her. *Go away, Uncle Ralph,* she said silently. *Don't spy on me.*

But it wasn't Uncle Ralph at the shore end of the pier. A little boy stood there. He had big eyes and a solemn face, and he wore an old-fashioned sailor suit with short pants and a broad collar.

A little kid, Chris marveled. *Out here in the woods, all by himself. He must be lost.*

"Hi," she shouted and started to scramble to her feet. But just then the sun peeked out from behind a cloud bank, and the pier, the lawn, and the house itself were swallowed up in a glittering flash. Chris blinked. When the light returned to normal, she blinked again.

The boy was gone. It was as if he'd never been there at all.

3.

The Ghost Boy

Chris looked up and down the shore. Here was where the boy had stood, at the joining of the pier to the beach. She was sure of it. Yet there were no footprints in the sand.

Maybe he was too light to leave prints. But where could he have come from? And where had he gone?

She hurried back to the house. A few minutes before, she'd promised herself that she wouldn't speak to Uncle Ralph again unless he spoke to her first. But this was an emergency.

Her uncle was coming down the stairs as she burst through the front door.

"Uncle Ralph," she began, "there's a little boy out there. I mean, there *was* a little boy, but now he's gone!

I'm afraid he's lost—"

"Christina." Uncle Ralph's voice was calm, as if he'd made up his mind to keep it that way. "I happen to know there isn't another house on this side of the lake. And there are no paths—nothing but the road we followed in from the highway." He looked at her sternly. "It's all right to make believe, as long as you know what's true and what's not."

Chris clenched her fists. She knew the difference between truth and make-believe. "I saw him! I did! Maybe—maybe he was a ghost!"

Uncle Ralph sighed. "Come into the study, Christina," he said. "We're going to have a little talk."

Feet dragging, Chris went with him. *A ghost,* she thought. Why had she said that? It was a silly idea, and just the kind of thing Uncle Ralph would expect of her.

Her uncle sat down behind the big desk and motioned her into the chair across from him. It was like being called to the principal's office at school.

"Now, Christina." He even sounded like a principal. "I know you don't want to be here with me. You realize I'm not exactly thrilled with the situation either. I'm not used to having a child around—"

"I'm ten years old," Chris interrupted. "And there's a *little* child out there! He must be lost."

"Still, we both have to make the best of it," he went

on. "We have to get along until Ma—your grand-mother—is home from the hospital. Which, I surely hope, will be soon. When that happens, you can go back to the farm and keep her company."

Chris tried not to look impatient. She wanted to go outside and search for the boy.

"I know you think I'm a stuffy old bird," Uncle Ralph said. "You may be right, but I am the way I am. I don't like roughnecks—boys *or* girls. I like things quiet and orderly. I've decided that if we're going to keep from driving each other crazy, we'll have to be pretty independent. Do you know what that means?"

Chris nodded. "I can take care of myself. I *like* to take care of myself."

Uncle Ralph forced a smile. "Well, then, that's fine," he said. "I have work to do this summer—research and writing—so I'll be spending most of my time here in this room. You can just . . . just explore and have a great time by yourself. I'll be here if you need me," he added. It was clear that he hoped she wouldn't need him, ever.

Chris stood up. Darkness had curtained the windows.

"Of course we'll eat together," Uncle Ralph said. He looked at Chris anxiously. "You don't have a sensitive stomach, do you? I mean, besides getting carsick. I'm not much of a cook."

"I eat anything," Chris told him.

"Good." He seemed to be trying to be friendly, now that they'd had their little talk. "I'll be in frequent touch with the hospital in Rochester. As soon as your grandmother's ready for company, we'll drive down to see her."

"Fine."

"Then everything's clear?"

"Sure."

It seemed to Chris that Uncle Ralph's desk was about a mile wide. Over there on the other side was a calm, neat world where people did the right thing without even thinking about it. Uncle Ralph belonged there, and Aunt Grace. Jenny belonged there, too. But not Chris. She belonged on this side of the desk, where unexpected things happened. Adventures. Mysteries. Maybe even ghosts!

"See you later," she said, so cheerfully that Uncle Ralph raised an eyebrow. She darted through the dining room to the foyer and out the front door.

Night had closed in. Beyond the dark lawn, the beginnings of a moon path stretched across the water.

Darn it, Chris thought. *I'm too late.*

But her disappointment lasted only a moment. She would see the little boy again. She would! If he were real, she'd solve the mystery of where he'd come from.

If he were a ghost—she shivered, not believing—if he were a ghost, that would be the scariest thing that had ever happened to Christina Joan Cooper. She wondered if she could bear it.

4.

A Warning from the Attic

The telephone was ringing when Chris came downstairs the next morning. Uncle Ralph was still in his room.

"Chrissy, is that you?" Mrs. Cooper's voice was warm and anxious. She might have been right there in the gloomy hallway instead of thousands of miles away in Alaska.

"Mom!" The word came out in a little gasp.

"How *are* you, sweetie? We had a terrible time getting your number. I called Aunt Grace first, and she finally found it in Grandma's phone book. Uncle Ralph must have sent it to her when he found out where he was going to be for the summer. We were so sorry to hear about Grandma's surgery."

Chris cleared her throat. "She's doing okay, I guess."

"That's what Aunt Grace said. And how about you, dear? How are you and Uncle Ralph getting along? Are you staying in a nice place?"

"It's fine." Yesterday, in Grandma's front yard, Chris would have given anything in the world to be able to tell her parents just how miserable she was. Now that she had a chance to do it, the words wouldn't come. There was nothing they could do to help, way off in Alaska, and besides, she had something exciting to think about now. She had a mystery to solve.

"Well, I'm glad. Daddy's very busy, but we're going to do some sightseeing, too. It would certainly put a damper on the whole trip if we thought you and Jenny weren't having some good times."

Uncle Ralph started down the stairs and stopped short when he saw Chris at the telephone.

"It's my mom," Chris said. "I guess you want to talk to her."

He moved in very slow motion down the rest of the stairs. "I guess I do," he said. "Hello, Jean?" He listened for a minute, screwing his face into funny grimaces. Chris knew her mother must be apologizing for burdening Ralph and Grace. Uncle Ralph would be thinking about how he and Aunt Grace had argued about who was to take the children. His lips were clamped shut, but he was probably wishing he could tell his sister to come home at once and look after her kids herself.

When he spoke at last, his voice was tightly controlled. "We'll manage," he said. "Don't worry about it. Christina and I have had a talk, and we understand each other." He paused again. "No, no, everything is all right. Do you want to speak to her again?"

Chris took the phone and listened to her mother's beloved voice, edged now with concern. "Uncle Ralph sounds tense," she said. "I'm afraid you'll have to go your own way as much as possible, dear. Find something interesting to do—that's the answer. Find a project."

Chris nodded into the phone. "I have one, Mom," she said. "Don't worry, I'm okay." She wished she could tell her mother about the little boy, but she didn't dare; Uncle Ralph was probably listening to every word.

By the time they said good-bye, he had the table set for breakfast in the kitchen. Rain was falling in a gray sheet beyond the open back door, and the room was dim in spite of the overhead light.

"I hope you don't expect eggs and bacon and that sort of thing for breakfast," Uncle Ralph said. He looked as if his mind were still on the telephone conversation.

"Cereal's fine," Chris said. She pictured the farm breakfast she'd be having if she were at Grandma's house. Pancakes, maybe, and bacon and warm syrup. Maggie would be under the table, poking Chris's toe with her nose to remind her that someone down there was waiting for scraps.

Uncle Ralph looked out at the rain and scowled. "With that going on, I don't suppose you can play outside today."

"I wasn't going to *play,* anyway," Chris retorted. "I was going to look for—I was going to explore. As long as it's raining, I'll explore the house."

Uncle Ralph nodded. "Good. Just don't break anything."

They were like strangers, stiff and polite. *Well,* Chris thought, *that's just what we are—strangers. It's the way I told Aunt Grace it would be. He doesn't want to know me, and I don't want to know him.*

As soon as she'd finished her cereal and orange juice, Chris scooted back upstairs to her bedroom. She'd chosen it the night before, after opening several doors of rooms full of heavy furniture, thick, musty carpets, and velvet draperies. This room must have been the housekeeper's. It looked more like home, with simple, white-painted furniture and a faded rag rug.

Hurriedly, Chris smoothed her sheets and blanket and arranged the white spread with as few wrinkles as possible. The contents of her duffel bag were on the dresser top and the floor. She gathered things in armfuls and dumped them into the dresser drawers. *There,* she thought. *Let him come poking around.* He'd see that she could be as neat as anybody else when she chose to be.

She heard Uncle Ralph cross the foyer and go to his study. As soon as the door closed, she ran downstairs to the kitchen. The house keys were hanging on a hook next to the back door.

The night before, Chris had discovered one locked door among those she'd tried. It might be nothing but a storage closet, she supposed, but then why lock it? A good explorer would find out.

The locked room was next to her own. Chris shivered as she tried one key and then another; the hallway was chilly and damp. At last a key turned in the lock, and the door swung open.

She stepped into a room so different that it seemed part of another world. The floor was covered with a bright red carpet. Most of the furniture was maple and child-sized. Huge posters of real animals and of Mickey Mouse and Donald Duck covered the walls, except where floor-to-ceiling shelves were crowded with picture books, toy cars, and game boxes.

It was a wonderfully happy room—the only happy room Chris had found.

She tiptoed across the carpet to the little bed. The covers were neatly folded back, as if waiting for someone. The sheets and pillowcases were yellowed with age.

She went to the closet. A low rod held shorts and shirts and a shiny rain slicker. Chris pushed back some of the clothes and pulled out a pale blue sailor suit. She stared at it, trembling, and then thrust it back on the rack.

A sailor suit was what the little boy had been wearing last night. *Just like this one,* Chris thought, and for a moment she let herself believe the impossible. This was the little boy's room. Long ago, he'd lived in this house. He was still here, somewhere, watching!

She slammed the closet door. It couldn't be true. She was "getting things into a muddle," just as Uncle Ralph had said on their way to Grandma's house.

She moved to the book-and-toy shelf. Most of the books and games were too babyish to interest her, but on the bottom shelf she discovered a stack of comic books. Just what she liked! She picked up the top one and thumbed through it, looking for a Jokes and Riddles page.

"What did the monkey say when he caught his tail in the lawn mower?" Her voice was loud in the silent room. Quickly, she turned the book upside down to find the answer at the bottom.

"It won't be long now." She giggled. A small sound, like a sigh, made her turn to the door. The little boy stood there, smiling wistfully.

Chris couldn't believe it. Where had he come from?
How could he have gotten in without making a sound?
She tried to say hello, but the word came out in a
froggy croak.

The little boy vanished.

Chris darted to the door. "Come back, boy," she
called. "You don't have to be afraid." She ran down
the hall, stopping to open each closed door. The rooms
were empty.

At the end of the hall was a door she hadn't tried
the night before. She ran to it now and threw it open.
Stairs led upward into attic shadows. A blast of icy air
struck her as she mounted the first step.

Go! Go away! The words thundered around Chris,
a terrible rush and roar that was partly sound, partly
frigid cold. She leaped back into the hall and slammed
the door with all her strength. In the quiet that followed,
she could hear her heart thudding.

She leaned against the wall. At the other end of the
hall, her bedroom door stood open, offering safety, but
her legs wouldn't carry her there. *What had happened?*
she wondered numbly. What was there, on the other
side of the attic door? She'd felt as if she were drowning
in that avalanche of sound and chilling wind.

She took a shaky step, then raced to the stairs and
down to the front door, her feet pounding furiously.

"What's all the racket?" Uncle Ralph shouted from his study, but she kept on running, letting the door slam behind her. *Go away!* the voice from the attic had told her, and that was what she wanted to do.

The trouble was, she realized when she reached the end of the pier, there was no place to hide when she stopped running.

5.

The Boy Comes Back

Chris sat on the pier for a long time, watching the raindrops hit the lake in overlapping ripples. The air was warm, and the rain soothed her. By the time it had slowed to a drizzle, she felt oddly comforted. The lake, the gentle rain, the line of still, green pines edging the water were more real than anything that had happened in the old house.

Maybe nothing did happen, she told herself. A cold wind—was that so scary? And had she really heard a voice telling her to go away? She couldn't be sure. *Maybe I even made up the little boy,* she thought, trying hard to believe it was true. *When people are lonesome, they sometimes make up a friend.*

True or not, she didn't want to go back to the house, at least until Uncle Ralph finished working and came out of his study. Even his disapproving company would be better than none.

Find something interesting to do—that's the answer. Find a project. Chris sat up straight. That was what her mother had told her on the telephone, and Chris had agreed, planning then to find out more about the little boy. Now she decided she wanted to forget him. She'd find another project. *Don't sit around and mope,* was what her mother always advised. *Get going!*

Chris narrowed her eyes and looked out over the gray water. What could she do? What would keep her busy during the long hours while Uncle Ralph was working? What would keep her out of that house?

Suddenly she had the answer. She would teach herself how to swim.

Chris had taken lessons at the YWCA at home, and she could paddle around a little, but she'd never been able to build up to real distances. Now was the perfect time to learn. If she stayed in shallow water all the time, Uncle Ralph couldn't object. And by the time her parents came home, she'd be an expert. She might even be a lifeguard some day.

She kicked off her sneakers and slid into the clear brown water. It barely reached her shorts. Carefully, she waded across the sandy bottom, heading toward the little point of land that marked the end of the lawn. The water was waist-deep; she could see the bottom all the way, and there were no holes or drop-offs to worry about. This would be her practice course every day.

That afternoon, and for the two days following, Chris worked hard, with disappointing results. She could swim barely half the distance from the pier to the point without standing up. Over and over she tried, until her arms and legs ached and she puffed like a steam engine. At night she could hardly stay awake through supper, and afterward she dozed in a chair while Uncle Ralph read.

"What's the matter with you?" he asked toward the end of the week, when she yawned noisily at the table. "I thought you were the top that never stopped turning."

"I'm learning to swim," Chris told him. "In very shallow water." She wanted to reassure him right away so he wouldn't object. She needed this project. Swimming tired her out. She didn't lie awake at night listening for noises in the attic, and she had less time to watch for the little boy.

The next morning, a remarkable thing happened. From the moment Chris slid off the end of the pier, she felt confident. Her arms and legs moved, smoothly, crisply, through the water. She raised her head to gulp air in an easy rhythm. Almost before she knew it, she was at the point and scrambling up on the beach.

I did it! She rolled over and lay back, exultant. *I wish Jenny was here.* She wanted someone to share this good moment.

When she sat up, the little boy was standing at the end of the pier. The pale blue sailor suit was the color of the sky. As she stared, he raised a hand in greeting.

He was there! She hadn't made him up, after all. He was there, and he'd watched her as she swam.

"Hi!" Chris shouted. "Wait there. Please! I'm coming back."

She jumped up and waded into the water, her eyes on the little figure. "Watch this!" she shouted and plunged forward to show him how well she could do.

When she stood up again, seconds later, the pier was empty.

A cloud passed over the sun. Chris's legs buckled, and she sat down on the sandy bottom, shivering. He couldn't have run away that fast. It wasn't possible. The pier was too long, and beyond it lay an expanse of lawn with no place to hide. Maybe he'd fallen into the water on the other side. Panicked, she began swimming again, moving faster than she would have thought possible. On the far side of the pier, she stood up and waded quickly through the shallow water.

He wasn't there.

When she reached the shore, she looked up and down the beach one more time, then sat down on the narrow strip of sand. A sun-warmed breeze dried her, and the goose bumps gradually faded from her arms. Still, she couldn't stop shaking.

Think good thoughts! she ordered herself. Think about her bedroom at home with its cheerful clutter. Think about her last birthday, when her mother had invited three friends for a surprise sleep-over party. Think about . . . but it was no use. All she could think about was the little boy.

I've seen a ghost. The wonder of that was almost too much to bear. She'd seen a ghost, and the ghost looked like somebody's nice little brother. Then why was she afraid? He was just a little kid, and he was lonesome—she was sure of that. Surely he hadn't come to frighten her; he'd come because he wanted a friend.

Gradually the shivering stopped, and she began to feel more excited than scared. This was an adventure. She pictured the little boy standing out on the pier, his hand raised, as if to congratulate her on how well she'd swum. And suddenly she knew she had to see him again. She wanted to help him.

How could she bring him back?

Chris thought about it all the rest of the day. She swiveled her head around so often, looking for the boy, that Uncle Ralph asked her if there was something the matter with her neck.

The next morning she was up early and outside, wandering restlessly around the yard. She walked along the shore, and all around the edge of the lawn, peering into the woods. When she reached the big garage behind the house, she hesitated, then tried the door. It opened into shadowy depths.

In the light from the tiny windows the garage loomed as large as a church. Some folding chairs hung from the walls, and on the far side a small boat was balanced on the rafters.

Chris started to back out before she noticed a board propped against one wall. It took a minute for her to realize it was a swing. The seat was sanded, and the heavy ropes were firmly tied.

Someone must have made it for the little boy but hadn't put it up. *Why not?* Chris wondered. She tugged the swing out into the sunshine, feeling as if she'd found what she'd been looking for.

Once again she circled the yard, this time searching for a tree with straight, sturdy branches. The best one was close to the shore. She hurried back to the garage and found a ladder to help her into the tree's lower branches. Then she pulled up the swing and tied it to the biggest branch, using knots her father had taught her.

The seat of the swing hung high, so she had to stand

on tiptoe to hitch herself onto it. Cautiously at first, to test the knots, then higher and higher she flew. With blue sky above her, sparkling water below, she felt as free as the eagle that sometimes soared over the lake in wide circles.

When the swing slowed to a stop, she was hardly surprised to see the little boy watching. He was at the edge of the woods, and his shy smile made her long to comfort him. *It's his swing,* she thought, *and I'm the one who's riding on it.* She smiled at him encouragingly, till he faded back into the shadows and was gone.

"You looked as if you were having a good time this morning," Uncle Ralph commented at lunch.

Chris glanced up, surprised. Most of the time she paged through comic books while she ate, because Uncle Ralph always brought a book to the table and seldom spoke.

"I saw you swinging," he explained. "I've been coming out occasionally to see how the swimming was going, but I got involved in something and I didn't see you put up the swing. You should have let me help you. Are you sure it's safe?"

"I know how to do stuff like that," Chris told him.

"Hmm." He looked at her, hard. "Still, I think I'll check after lunch."

Chris shrugged, annoyed. *I thought you didn't want*

to be bothered. She swallowed the words. After all, it was kind of nice to have him talk to her, since there was no one else around.

After lunch, she rinsed the dishes while Uncle Ralph went outside. When her work was finished, she dashed upstairs and peeked out of her bedroom window. Uncle Ralph was down at the lake front, straddling the branch that held the swing. One hand fingered the knots and tugged at the ropes; the other hand clutched a smaller branch overhead. When he was satisfied, he began edging backward, very slowly.

He's scared! Chris realized. Imagine a grown man afraid to climb out on a branch as sturdy as that one! She ducked back from the window and waited till she heard her uncle come in and return to his study.

For a few minutes this noon she'd thought about telling him some of the exciting discoveries of the last few days. She could have mentioned how well the swimming had gone yesterday morning. She could have told him about the rowboat stored in the garage. Now she was glad she'd kept still. He'd probably get nervous and be full of crabby "don't's" and warnings.

She didn't even consider telling him about the ghost boy, or about the dark presence on the other side of the attic door. When it came to ghosts, she *knew* what he'd say.

It would be different if he could see the ghost boy

himself, she thought. *But he won't. The boy comes when I'm feeling good. When I'm laughing. And Uncle Ralph doesn't laugh. The world really is too much for him—especially with Chris Cooper cluttering up his summer.*

6.

Footsteps in the Hall

Midnight. Chris peered at the straight-up, glowing hands of her clock. She didn't know what had awakened her. Maybe it was the baked beans and hash they'd had for supper. Uncle Ralph's meals came mostly from cans.

She tiptoed to the door and peeked out. Trembling, she felt for the light switch, hoping Uncle Ralph wouldn't wake up.

The hall was chilly and damp. At the far end, beyond the row of closed bedrooms, the attic door stood open.

What should she do? Call her uncle and tell him— what? *Wake up, Uncle Ralph. The attic door's open and I'm scared.* He would tell her to close it and go back to bed.

She started down the corridor, pressing close to the

wall. If there was some *thing* on those steps, she didn't want to see it. With every step, she felt colder. Her teeth chattered.

As she edged around the chest that stood just beyond the last bedroom door, there was a thud from above. It could have been a footstep. With a whimper of terror, Chris flung the attic door shut. Then she pulled the chest from its place against the wall and shoved it hard against the door.

Uncle Ralph's bedroom door shot open. "Christina! What in the world!"

Chris felt dizzy. "The door . . . open . . . " she gasped. "I—I closed it."

"You certainly did." Uncle Ralph looked disgusted. "But did you have to bang it? In the middle of the night? I thought the house was falling down around me." His gray hair stuck out in every direction. "Who cares if the attic door was open, anyway?"

Chris took a long, shuddering breath. "It gets cold."

Uncle Ralph pressed his head between his hands. "You have a very noisy way of dealing with cold," he said. "Did you ever think of just putting on an extra blanket?" He looked at the closed door with the chest in front of it, and then at Chris's white face. "Doors open and close by themselves in an old house," he said, a little more gently. "Happens all the time. Now, if you're ready to go back to bed, I am."

Chris padded down the hall to her room and switched on one of the dresser lamps. Then she closed the door and pulled a chair in front of it. A moment later she heard the hall light click off.

I'll stay awake until morning, she promised herself. *I won't close my eyes.*

But once in bed, with the covers tucked up to her ears, she slipped quickly into uneasy sleep. First she dreamed that her mother and father had been in a car accident. Then she dreamed that Aunt Grace was moving to Alaska and taking Jenny with her. And then she dreamed there was a tiger in her closet, struggling to get out.

"No!" She woke with the word straining her throat. The room was still dark except for the circle of light from the dresser lamp.

Out in the hall, something scraped across the floor. The chest! The chest was being pushed aside. Chris dived under the covers, but she couldn't close out the slow, heavy footsteps coming down the hall. As they drew closer, damp cold seeped into her bedroom.

He—it—was outside her door. She knew it. Uncle Ralph would be sorry tomorrow when he found her lying here, frozen solid, a look of terror on her face. *She looks so pitiful,* he'd say. *Why in the world didn't she get herself another blanket?*

The footsteps moved away.

Chris lay rigid, afraid to move. Time passed, and her muscles ached, but she stayed in her sheet-tent. When she peered out at last, the first gray light of morning was touching the windows.

She stayed in bed another half-hour, listening to the world wake itself up. A cardinal sang. A squirrel scolded. The lake made its soft, lapping sounds.

When she opened her bedroom door, the house was very still. Uncle Ralph's door was closed. The attic door was closed, too.

There was nothing unusual to see, except for the chest. It stood out from the attic door at an angle, as if it had been roughly thrust aside.

7.

Grandma's Hint

Uncle Ralph peered around the box of corn flakes. "I'm sorry I barked at you last night," he said. "You startled me."

"That's okay." Chris had been trying to decide whether to tell him about the pushed-aside chest. He might accuse her of moving it herself. He might get angry all over again.

The gray head was already bent over the book beside his plate. *He wouldn't want to know,* she decided. *He doesn't want to think about anything that isn't in a book.* But something scary was happening in this house. Something bad! She almost forgot to eat, trying to figure out what it was.

Uncle Ralph swallowed his last spoonful of cereal

and closed his book. "We're going to see your grandmother today," he said.

All thoughts of the attic door were swept away for the moment. "You're kidding!" Chris exclaimed. "Will she come home with us?"

"No, she won't. I called the hospital early this morning, and she said she's feeling much better. But the doctor wants her to stay a while longer. Her arthritis has been acting up, and he wants her to go through the arthritis clinic while she's there. It'll take a while."

Chris eyed him suspiciously. "How long?"

"A *while*, Christina. Maybe two weeks." He pushed back his chair and began picking up dishes. "Anyway, we're going to see her today," he said. "I thought you'd be thrilled to see someone beside your cranky old uncle."

"Oh, I am." Chris stopped, aware that she wasn't being tactful. "I mean—let's go this minute," she begged.

"After we wash the dishes and make our beds," Uncle Ralph said. "We don't want to come back to a mess."

Chris wouldn't have cared about that at all, but she kept still. She could hardly wait to see her grandmother. If she had to stay here for another two whole weeks, and she couldn't tell Uncle Ralph what was happening in the house, maybe Grandma would listen. She had always taken Chris's adventures seriously.

But by the time Chris and Uncle Ralph had found their way through the hospital lobby in Rochester, taken the elevator to the third floor, wandered down one long hall and then another, Chris didn't feel like talking at all. The hospital made her uneasy. People sat around in wheelchairs or walked up and down the halls in their bathrobes. All the nurses were in a hurry. And when they finally found Room 347, Grandma didn't look like the grandma Chris remembered. Her usually pink face was pale, and the glossy brown hair looked frizzy. Only her voice was the same.

"Chrissy! Ralph! Oh, I'm so glad to see you two dears." She held out her arms, and Chris ran into them. Then Grandma hugged and kissed Uncle Ralph. "You both look so good to me!" she exclaimed. "So healthy!"

"I've learned how to swim longer distances," Chris told her.

"Good for you!"

Uncle Ralph sat on the edge of the bed and took Grandma's hand. "How are you feeling, Ma?"

"Fine, except for the arthritis," Grandma said. "Bored. Hungry for my own cooking." She brushed off the rest of their questions, after telling them she was starting appointments at the arthritis clinic tomorrow. When her treatments were finished, she could go home. "And you'll be there," she said, giving Chris another squeeze. "You and Jenny will be my helpers till your folks come back. We'll have a grand time, just the way we planned."

"I can't wait!" Chris said. "Oh, I *wish* you could go home today."

There was a little silence. Uncle Ralph shuffled his feet. Grandma looked at him and then at Chris.

"I wonder if you'd run down to the gift shop and get me a magazine, Ralph," she said. "You know the kind I like. And a few chocolates, dear. With cherries, if they have them."

Uncle Ralph seemed pleased to have a job. He hurried off, and Grandma patted the bed beside her. "Sit here, Chrissy," she invited. "Now, how are things going? Tell me."

The words spilled out. "Uncle Ralph doesn't want me with him. Oh, we get along okay"—she wanted to chase away Grandma's worried frown—"but he'll be glad when I'm gone. And so will I," she added.

Grandma hugged her. "My Ralph is a loner, I'm afraid. He's lived by himself for a long time, and he's used to it. But I'm sure he's glad to have you with him, dear. I'm just sure of it! He's always been a good host when I've visited him in the city."

Chris sighed. "He loves you, Grandma. I think it's just tomboys he doesn't like."

"Of course he loves me," Grandma said. "But he

loves you, too, dear. It's just that he's the kind of man who'd rather *do* something for you than tell you his feelings."

Chris remembered Uncle Ralph crawling out on the branch to test her swing, even though he was afraid. She supposed that was what Grandma meant by "doing something."

"Anyway," Grandma went on, "Ralph is a very lonely person, Chrissy. Maybe you can bring a little sunshine into my boy's life while you're with him. What do you think?"

"I don't know," Chris said honestly. "I don't think he wants my kind of sunshine." But she knew she'd have to try, for Grandma's sake and for Uncle Ralph's, too. If he really was lonely, she wanted to help him.

There were footsteps in the hall, and Chris could hear Uncle Ralph talking to someone nearby. She had missed her chance to tell Grandma all about the strange happenings at the house.

"Grandma, what would you do if you wanted to find out about something that happened a long time ago?" she asked hurriedly. "Uncle Ralph says something bad happened in the house where we're staying, but he doesn't know what it was. I want to find out."

Grandma's eyes were on the door, watching eagerly for Uncle Ralph's return. "Well, I guess . . . I guess I'd look in old newspapers," she said. "You can go to the nearest library and—" Uncle Ralph hurried in. He carried a whole stack of magazines and a huge box of chocolates.

"There," he said, looking pleased as he stacked his purchases on the table next to the bed. "That should do it."

"Oh, my, yes," Grandma said. "Thank you, dear." She winked at Chris as she started to open the box of candy. "Love comes in all kinds of packages," she said. "Right, Chris?"

"Right," Chris said. She winked back, but her mind was busy with Grandma's good idea. *Look in old newspapers. . . .*

All she had to do now was get Uncle Ralph to stop at a library.

8.

"Murder—That's What Happened...."

"We'll stop at Clearwater on the way back," Uncle Ralph said as they walked to the car. "We're running low on powdered milk and a lot of other stuff. And then I want to go to the library. If they have one, that is."

Chris stared at him, wide-eyed. Could he read her mind? Had he overheard Grandma talking? No, she decided, he was just naturally a Library Person.

The grocery shopping went quickly, with Uncle Ralph tossing cans and packages and loaves of bread into their cart with hardly a glance at the labels. After that they went next door to a drugstore. Uncle Ralph bought shaving cream, and Chris found a paperback book full of jokes and riddles. If she was going to bring sunshine into her uncle's life, maybe the book would help.

And maybe not. He sniffed when he saw what she'd chosen.

"Now the library," he said. "It's right around the corner, according to the druggist. I don't suppose it's a very big one. . . ."

His voice faded as they turned off the main street and stared at the tiny one-room building marked *Public Library.* Uncle Ralph shook his head. "Not a chance in a million that they'll have anything I need," he grumped, "but I suppose they can order for me. I'll be out in a few minutes, Christina. You can wait in the car."

Chris felt sick with disappointment. She'd pictured a big two-story library like the one at home. How could she go into this little building and ask to see newspapers of thirty years ago? In the first place, they probably wouldn't have them. In the second place, Uncle Ralph would hear her and tell her to forget the whole thing.

She walked back to the corner and looked for something to do while she waited. Across the street was a clothing store advertising a sale of summer shorts and T-shirts. Beyond that was an ice-cream shop. *Chocolate, pecan, and rainbow,* she thought, suddenly starved. She'd take a triple-dipper back for Uncle Ralph, too.

She was just turning in to the shop when a sign in the next window caught her eye: *The Clearwater Journal.* A newspaper office! She studied the other signs taped to the glass. *Subscribe now! Job printing, reasonable rates.* Surely the printers would keep copies of their old newspapers.

The triple-dippers forgotten, Chris marched into the office and looked around. A skinny, glum-looking man was behind the counter. One fist clutched a telephone; with the other hand he was jotting additions to a long list of items. He had an odd, glazed expression, and his glance flicked over Chris without seeing her.

After what seemed a very long time, he mumbled a good-bye and hung up. "Liberated women," he snarled into the air above Chris's head.

"Excuse me?" She took one step closer to the counter.

"Women!" the man snapped. "Wives!"

Chris looked over her shoulder, ready to run if necessary.

"I suppose when you grow up you're going to want a *career,*" the man jeered. He made *career* sound terrible. "My wife's a nurse. Works second shift at the hospital."

Chris cleared her throat. "That's nice," she said cautiously.

"Nothing nice about it! She calls to tell me to do the

grocery shopping. She calls to tell me to wash the windows. She calls to tell me what to fix for dinner." He shook his head so hard the pencil poised behind one ear hurtled through the air. "And what do *you* want?"

"I'd like to see some . . . some old newspapers," Chris said. The request sounded silly, even to herself.

"How old?" The man glared at the phone as if he was daring it to ring again.

"About thirty years," Chris said. "If it isn't too much trouble."

"It's trouble," the man said. "What week do you want? We publish once a week."

"I—I don't know." Why had she thought this would work?

The man scooped up his pencil and thrust it back behind his ear. "Then I can't help you," he said, sounding pleased. "You certainly don't expect me to pull out a whole year's worth of papers, do you?"

That was exactly what Chris had hoped he'd do, but she didn't dare say so. Clearly, he didn't like females, even very young ones. Maybe he didn't like anybody.

She shifted from one foot to another. "I—we're staying at the old Charles house," she said. "It's a big house on a lake, way out in the woods. My uncle says something happened there about thirty years ago. I want to find out what it was."

The man scowled. "No need to get out a pack of newspapers to tell you that," he muttered. "Murders— that's what happened at the Charles house."

"Murders?"

"Two people—man and boy." The man pursed his lips. "It's not a *nice* story, and you shouldn't even want to know about it. You should be learning to cook. Or making doll clothes." He narrowed his eyes at her. "Nobody does what they're supposed to anymore. Nobody." He turned away and hunched over the list on his desk.

Chris waited. When he looked to see if she was still there, she forced a smile. "Just one paper, then," she pleaded. "Or two. That wouldn't be much trouble, would it?"

The man came back to the counter and glared down at her. "Do you want to know something?" he demanded. "You remind me of my wife. You women—" He turned away so fast that the pencil took off again and arced over the counter. "One paper," he said. "And that's all."

"That'll be fine," Chris said quickly. "Thanks a lot." *Now if he'll just hurry up,* she thought, *so I can read what it says before Uncle Ralph comes looking for me. . . .*

The man didn't hurry, but when he returned from the back room, Chris saw that he'd chosen the single newspaper with care. *CHARLES MURDERS SOLVED,* the headline said in big letters. Under it were several stories concerning the case.

Chris thanked him again and carried the paper to the window. She wanted to keep a lookout for Uncle Ralph while she read.

The first article was a background piece on the Charles family. They were wealthy Milwaukee people who had built the house on the lakeshore and lived there quietly for several years before their only child, Russell, was born. A grainy snapshot of Russell showed him wearing a rain slicker and helmet.

Early one spring Mr. and Mrs. Charles went to Europe on an extended business trip. They hired a tutor-companion named Thomas Dixon to stay with the boy while they were away. Six weeks later, Dixon and Russell were found shot to death in the big house.

The Charleses were brokenhearted. After their return from Europe, they stayed in the house only a couple of weeks, then closed it up and moved away from the painful memories it held.

A second article consisted of an interview with the sheriff after the capture of one of the murderers. The killer had confessed at once, admitting that he and Dixon and two other men had been involved in the theft of some extremely valuable stamps in New York.

Dixon had run away, taking the rarest stamps with him and leaving his partners with little to show for their crime. He'd taken the position with the Charles family in order to hide out for a while. When the furious thieves caught up with him, he'd refused to tell them where the stamps were hidden. They had killed him, then killed the little boy as well, because he'd seen and heard too much.

Chris read as fast as she could. According to the sheriff, the stamps still had not been found, and he thought they were gone for good. Dixon might have sold them on his way to the Midwest; he might even have lost them or destroyed them.

She glanced up. Uncle Ralph was just coming around the corner. He looked both ways, then turned and started up the street in the other direction. She hurried back to the counter, scooping up the man's pencil on the way.

"Here's the paper," she said. "Thanks again."

The man was at his desk, glaring at his list as if it might bite him. When he looked up, his expression was mournful.

"I bet you never played with a doll in your life," he said. "Nobody does what they're supposed to anymore."

Chris rolled the pencil across the counter and darted

to the door. "Good-bye," she called over her shoulder and ran outside before he could accuse her of anything else.

Halfway up the next block and on the other side of the street, Uncle Ralph was peering into windows. His shoulders were hunched with annoyance as he hunted for her, and Chris knew he would agree with the man in the newspaper office. *Nobody does what they're supposed to anymore.*

She hurried next door and ordered two ice-cream cones, hopping from one foot to the other while she waited for the clerk to ring up the sale.

"I told you to wait in the car," Uncle Ralph said when Chris caught up to him at last. But he cut the scolding short when she handed him his triple-decker cone.

Meekly, she followed him to the car. Her head was whirling with all she'd learned in the last few minutes. *Russell Charles,* she thought. *That's his name. And he is really and truly a ghost.* She even knew when he had died. And she could make a guess about the terrifying presence in the attic. *It's Thomas Dixon up there,* she thought. The ghost of a man who stole the stamps and then cheated his partners. The ghost of the man who was responsible for Russell Charles having been murdered.

9.

A Faint, Smiling Figure

"Why does a tall man eat less than a short one?" Chris sat at the end of the pier and read the riddle in a loud voice. She flipped to the back of her paperback for the answer.

"Because he makes a little go a long way!" She twisted around, hoping to catch sight of little Russell Charles, but the shore was deserted.

"Why does a spider spin a web?" She paused. "Because she can't knit!"

She giggled at the idea of a spider with eight knitting needles. And suddenly Russell was there, a faint, smiling figure under a tall birch. Almost at once he was gone, but Chris was thrilled. She'd made him appear. Her laughter had brought him.

Poor little kid. He'd had nobody to laugh with for years and years.

She started back to the house. On the way she picked some of the feathery blue flowers that grew in the tall grass edging the lawn. If she were going to bring sunshine into Uncle Ralph's life, flowers might help.

The table was set—the blue bouquet, peanut butter, jelly, bread, tall glasses of milk—when Uncle Ralph came out of the study. He grunted, sat down, and opened his book.

"What do you think is worse than finding a juicy green worm in an apple, Uncle Ralph?" Chris had the paperback open on her lap.

Uncle Ralph looked up. "What kind of question is that?"

"It's a riddle," Chris explained. "You're supposed to guess the answer."

He thought for a minute and then shrugged. "I have no idea, Christina. Riddles aren't my thing. Sorry." He went back to his book.

"Half a worm," Chris said.

He looked up again. "Half a worm what?"

"It's worse to find half a worm in your apple than to find a whole one. If you find half of one, it means—"

Uncle Ralph groaned. "Yes, yes, I see what it means. Please don't explain."

Chris didn't mind the groan. Everyone groaned at

riddles. She glanced down at the paperback again. "Which is the left side of a round coconut cake?"

Now Uncle Ralph shook his head impatiently. "I told you, riddles aren't my thing. And I'd really like to finish this chapter, if it's okay with you." He began reading without waiting for a reply.

Chris's face felt hot. She made a double-decker peanut butter and jelly sandwich and ate it fast. Bringing sunshine into Uncle Ralph's life was a real pain.

She was leaving the kitchen when Uncle Ralph closed his book. He gestured at the jelly-glass bouquet. "You'd better throw out those weeds, Christina. They'll soon start to smell."

Weeds! She saw that the blue flowers had closed up tight in the last few minutes, leaving nothing but a cluster of stems. She grabbed the glass and emptied it out the back door, wishing she could punch someone.

She muttered to herself most of the afternoon. It took a long swim—to the point and back without stopping—to make her feel better. Let Uncle Ralph have his stuffy books, she decided. Let him be Mr. Sourpuss for the rest of his life, if that was what he wanted. Grandma would have to understand that she'd tried and failed.

But then Uncle Ralph surprised her. "Well," he said that evening as they sat down to canned chili, "which is it?"

"Which is what?"

"Which is the left side of a round coconut cake?"

"Oh." Chris wrinkled her nose. "You don't care," she said. "You really don't want to know."

"Right on the first point, wrong on the second," Uncle Ralph told her. "I don't care, and yet I do want you to tell me. I kept thinking about it this afternoon when my mind should have been on the paper I'm writing. It was annoying—like a mosquito buzzing around when you're trying to work."

"Well," Chris said reluctantly, "it's the part of the cake you haven't eaten yet. See, if it isn't eaten, it's left—"

"Stop!" He shook his head. "Don't explain." But he was smiling, and even though he kept his eyes on his book during the rest of the meal, Chris felt better. A smile was something.

"I'll make lunch tomorrow," she offered. She'd seen a bottle of maple syrup in Uncle Ralph's shopping cart, so there must have been pancake mix there, too. Pancakes should be easy.

But when she went to the kitchen the next noon, there was no mix. She searched the cupboards, finally deciding she'd have to make the pancakes her mother's way. She put some flour into a bowl, added milk, then broke an egg into the mixture. What else? She was pretty sure her mother added other things, but she couldn't remember what they were. Maybe a little sugar for flavor, she decided.

The batter was the right thickness and color. Chris put the skillet on the stove and dropped in a big dollop of butter. *Just wait till he sees this,* she thought, as the butter sputtered and browned. *He thinks I don't know how to make anything but trouble.*

When Uncle Ralph came out to the kitchen a few minutes later, she was just lifting the last pancake to the platter. Because he was watching, she gave it a little extra flip. The pancake flew through the air and landed on the floor.

Before he could stop himself, Uncle Ralph had stepped on it. He slid to one knee. "What's this?" he grumbled. He picked up the pancake as if it were a dead mouse.

Chris stared. The pancake was undamaged. There wasn't even a dent where Uncle Ralph had stepped on it.

"It's a—it's a pancake," she mumbled. "A surprise."

Uncle Ralph sat down, his eyes on the platter heaped with pancakes. "That was a nice thought," he said, sounding strained.

"They may be a little bit . . . stiff," Chris said. "But if you use lots of butter and lots of syrup. . . ." She gulped. "I'll show you."

She put a pancake on her plate, dropped a pat of

butter on it, and poured on maple syrup. "Like this,"
she said, and took a big, dripping bite.

"Ugh!" The pancake was like leather in her mouth.
Watching her expression, Uncle Ralph began to laugh.
He went on laughing while she chewed and chewed.

"Give up, Christina," he advised when he could get
his breath. "It isn't going to go down."

Chris ran to the sink and spit out the pancake. When
she looked up, Russell Charles was at the window. He
smiled in at them and then he was gone.

Chris whirled. "Did you see?" she asked. "Did you
see him, Uncle Ralph?"

"See whom?" Uncle Ralph said. "Is this another
riddle?"

Chris opened her mouth and closed it. Uncle Ralph
was still chuckling, but his smile would fade in a hurry
if she told him a ghost had been enjoying his laughter.

"It's not a riddle," she said. "I'm sorry about the
pancakes."

Uncle Ralph went to the refrigerator. "How about
French toast?" he asked. "As long as the syrup's on
the table."

"Okay." Chris watched the window, but Russell didn't
return. She dumped the pancakes into the garbage can
while Uncle Ralph mixed eggs and milk for the French
toast.

"Maybe I just threw away a great invention," she

said when they'd returned to the table. "Those pancakes might have been terrific for patching old shoes. Or for fixing holes in the roof."

To her amazement, Uncle Ralph leaned across the table and patted her arm. "You're a good sport, Christina," he said. "I'm sorry I laughed. But it *was* funny. The look on your face...."

She could have told him it was worth making the world's worst pancakes if they made him laugh out loud. But she didn't say it. Bringing sunshine into another person's life was tricky enough without that person knowing what you were up to.

10.

"You Mean He's a Ghost?"

A book could change your life, Chris discovered. Of course, Uncle Ralph still groaned every time she opened her paperback, but he listened to the riddles. Once in a while, he even guessed the right answer. Afterward, they talked about other things as well.

"You're a rare one, Christina," he said one day, but it didn't sound as if he was criticizing her. Actually, Chris thought, it wasn't just the riddles that were making the difference. Uncle Ralph had changed since the great pancake disaster. Chris caught him looking at her with amusement, as if he'd just noticed she was a real person, something more than a tomboy pest.

She could hardly wait to tell Grandma.

One evening, when mist rolled in off the lake and the air turned chilly, Uncle Ralph built a fire in the study fireplace. Chris sat cross-legged on the floor, enjoying the coziness of firelight and crackling logs.

"What kind of train will make you put on your glasses?" she read from her book.

Uncle Ralph scowled. "Ridiculous question."

"Eyestrain. Get it?" She snickered at his pained expression.

"They're becoming worse every day," Uncle Ralph said. "How many riddles are there in that blasted book?"

Chris looked at the cover. "Five hundred."

Uncle Ralph pretended to pull his hair. "I'll never live through them!" he exclaimed. "Five hundred of the most annoying—"

Chris giggled. "Did you buy any cocoa, Uncle Ralph? I could make us some."

"Certainly I bought cocoa," Uncle Ralph retorted. He raised an eyebrow at her. "How good are you at cocoa making, compared to pancake making, that is?"

"I'm terrif—" Chris stopped short. Across the study, and well outside the circle of firelight, Russell Charles stood watching.

"Uncle Ralph." She tried to keep her voice steady. "Uncle Ralph, look over there, in front of the closet door. Please, just look."

Uncle Ralph looked. For what seemed a very long time, Chris held her breath as they both stared at the little wavering figure. Then a log snapped, sending a shower of sparks up the chimney.

"Who's there?" Uncle Ralph exploded. He hurtled across the study and threw open the closet door. "Where is he?" he roared. "Where did he go? Christina!" He turned back from the empty closet. "What kind of trick was that?"

"It wasn't a trick," Chris told him. "It was Russell Charles. He lived in this house a long time ago. I've seen him lots of times."

Uncle Ralph shook his head as if were trying to wake himself from a dream. "You mean he's a ghost?" he said. "That's what you want me to believe?" He jumped up to look again into the closet. When he came back to the fire, his face was as pale as the little boy's had been.

"I don't *believe* in ghosts, Christina," he said. "I don't know what that—that thing was standing there, but it wasn't a ghost."

"Yes, it was," Chris insisted. "I saw him the very first day we got here, Uncle Ralph. I tried to tell you about him then, remember?"

The words tumbled over each other as she described the other times she'd seen Russell, and how she'd learned he liked being around someone who was cheerful. "He's lonesome," she said. "And I think he's scared, too."

"This is ridiculous." Uncle Ralph's glance kept returning to the corner where Russell had stood. "Scared of what?"

"Scared of whatever's in the attic," Chris told him. "There's something really bad up there."

Uncle Ralph took a handkerchief from his pocket and patted his forehead. "Something bad," he repeated. And when Chris hesitated, he leaned forward impatiently. "Go *on,*" he said. "You might as well tell me."

Chris described how the attic door had opened by itself, even with the chest pushed in front of it. She told about the footsteps, and the terrifying cold. And then she repeated what she'd learned in the office of *The Clearwater Journal.* "I think the ghost of the little boy's tutor is up there in the attic," she said. "His name is Thomas Dixon, and he was an awful person. Russell must be scared of him." She almost said "scared to death," but that wouldn't have made much sense.

Uncle Ralph leaned back in his chair and gave her a weak grin. "You really are something," he murmured. "Worked it all out, haven't you? Do you realize, Christina, that this is exactly how myths and fairy tales began?"

Chris frowned. "What do you mean?"

"I mean that all through the ages people have taken

facts—in this case, the unfortunate murders of two people—and added fantasy to make the facts more interesting. You're doing that now. You've discovered we're living in a house where two murders took place a long time ago, and now you're seeing the ghosts of the victims."

Chris clenched her teeth. "You saw Russell, too," she gritted.

"I saw something—a trick of the firelight—"

"A little boy! You saw him!"

"All right, I saw something that looked like a little boy. But there has to be some reasonable explanation— I just haven't thought of it yet. So let's not get into a state, okay?"

"I am not in a state!" Chris jumped up. Just when she was beginning to like Uncle Ralph, he had to act like—like the old Uncle Ralph. "I'm not lying either," she raged.

Uncle Ralph held up a calming hand. "I'm not calling you a liar," he said. "I know you *think* you've been seeing a ghost. Or ghosts." He closed his eyes as if he were suddenly tired of the whole subject. "Let's forget it. Why don't you make that cocoa now?"

"I don't want cocoa," Chris snapped. "I'm going to bed."

"No cocoa?" Uncle Ralph shook his head in dismay. For a moment his mock-mournful expression reminded her of the man in the newspaper office.

"I don't cook, and I'm glad of it," she announced, her voice squeaking with annoyance. "And you know what else? I'm going to have a career when I grow up."

Uncle Ralph followed her to the foyer and watched her go up the stairs. "What's that all about?" he asked. He was still standing there when she slammed her bedroom door hard behind her.

11.

"Someone—Something— in the Attic"

Chris lay across her bed and fought back tears. It was too early for sleep—only eight-thirty—but she wasn't going downstairs again. Every time she thought of Uncle Ralph sitting there smiling at her in that superior way, she gritted her teeth.

How could he refuse to believe in Russell Charles when he had seen him? If he wouldn't believe his own eyes, what would convince him? For just a moment, she considered calling him upstairs and then opening the attic door. Maybe if he felt that dead-cold rush of air. . . .

And what if he didn't feel it? What if she dragged him down the hall, threw open the attic door, and

nothing happened? No cold, no wind, no voice warning
them to go away. How he'd laugh then! How he'd tease
her!

She rolled over on her side and put a pillow over
her head. *Think good thoughts. Think about Grandma
getting better. Think about being a lifeguard some day.
Think about—*

The pillow must have kept her from hearing the
telephone. Suddenly a shaft of light cut across the room
and she sat up. Uncle Ralph was at the door, squinting
into the dark.

"On your feet, Christina," he said. "Telephone call—
from Alaska!"

Think about Mom and Dad! Chris shouted with joy
and flew across the room. She nearly knocked Uncle
Ralph over in her haste to get down the stairs to the
telephone in the hall.

"Chris, dear, are you there?" This time, her mother's
voice sounded very far off. "How are you, sweetie?
Are you and Uncle Ralph managing all right?"

"Oh, Mom—" Chris didn't know where to begin.
It seemed as if her mother must have known, somehow,
how much she needed a loving voice right now. "I'm
glad you called!"

"We think about you and Jenny so much." The telephone line crackled fiercely. "You *are* having fun, aren't

you, dear?" There was a pause, while her mother waited for Chris to say something. "Are you there, hon?"

Chris wondered if Uncle Ralph was at the top of the stairs listening to her part of the conversation. She realized that talking about their problems would be like tattling—and what could her folks do if she told them? She couldn't expect them to come racing home just because Chris believed in ghosts and Uncle Ralph didn't.

"I'm fine, Mom," Chris said. "Are you and Daddy having a good time?"

"Absolutely marvelous. We're taking lots of pictures so we can share it all with you and Jenny. And we're picking up some pretty nice presents, too. . . . What are you doing to enjoy yourself, Chrissy?"

"I'm swimming every day," Chris said, glad to have something she could talk about freely. "And I'm getting really good. I go exploring. And I'm really tanned."

There was more crackling on the line, and Chris's father boomed a greeting. "We miss you, Chris," he said, shouting, as he always did when he talked on the telephone. "Take care of yourself, kiddo. And tell Ralph not to spend all his time with his nose in a book. I hope you're making things lively for him."

"Sure, Dad."

Chris wondered if her parents had talked to Uncle Ralph about her before he called her to the phone.

Maybe he'd told them she was making up wild stories. She thought about it and decided that he wouldn't do that. He wouldn't like tattling any more than she did.

They said good-bye, and Chris put the telephone back on the hook. It had been wonderful to talk to them. Now that they were gone, she was more alone than ever, but she no longer felt like crying. Even if they hadn't said it in so many words, her parents had let her know how much they loved her. Just the way she was. If she'd told them about the ghosts, they wouldn't have laughed.

A floorboard creaked behind her, and Chris whirled around. Uncle Ralph was standing on the stairs. His face was a peculiar grayish-white, and as Chris stared, he sat down on a step with a thump. He looked the way Chris's father had looked last summer, after she and Jenny had persuaded him to go with them on the roller coaster. He looked frightened to death.

"Wh-what's the matter?"

He cleared his throat. "Someone—something—in the attic," he said, in a low voice. "I heard footsteps— while you were talking."

"Oh," Chris said. She put her hand on the telephone, as if she could bring her mother and father back again.

"I'd think it was a tramp—someone who sneaked in—except"—he ran his fingers through his gray hair— "except that it's getting very cold upstairs. Colder by the minute. I don't understand it."

Chris gulped. "I told you—" she began, but he interrupted irritably.

"Don't say I-told-you-so. It's very rude." He leaned forward tensely. "We have to do something, I suppose."

"Do what?"

"Find out what's going on. We'll have to look around up there."

"Not now!" Chris protested. "Not tonight, Uncle Ralph!"

But he was on his feet again and looking up the stairs. "Now," he insisted. "You may have nerves of steel, Christina, but I haven't. I can't just go to bed if there's something prowling around overhead or walking up and down outside my bedroom door."

A wave of relief washed over Chris. "You believe me now," she said. "You do, don't you?"

Uncle Ralph turned away from her and started up the stairs. "I didn't say that," he told her tightly.

Chris shivered. She could actually feel fear in the air around her. "Please, let's not go up there," she begged. "Russell Charles doesn't want us to." But she might as well have kept still. Uncle Ralph was already at the top of the stairs, and there was nothing to do but follow him.

12.

Behind the Attic Door

The air in the upstairs hall was both cold and clammy. Uncle Ralph waited for Chris to catch up with him. Then he strode down the hall.

"Promise me you'll never tell anybody about this— this ghost hunt," he said. "I can't believe I'm taking it seriously."

Chris gave his sweater a little tug. "We can wait until tomorrow morning," she said. "It's okay with me."

"Well, it's not okay with me." He put his hand on the knob of the attic door. "You can stay down here if you want to," he said. "I'll just go up and take a quick look—"

He turned the knob. The door flew open and crashed against the wall. An icy blast poured into the hall.

"What's this!" Uncle Ralph staggered backward. Chris flattened herself against the wall, trying to escape the icy fingers that tore at her clothes.

Uncle Ralph grabbed the door frame to steady himself. "Stay where you are, Christina," he bellowed over the roar of the wind. "I'm going up."

"Wait for me!" Chris's cry was lost in the gale, but she wasn't going to let Uncle Ralph out of her sight.

As they mounted the first steps, the rush of air grew even stronger. Chris clutched the banister with both hands. Uncle Ralph switched on his flashlight and pointed the beam toward the top of the stairs.

Crouching against the wind, Chris peered around him. At first she saw nothing but leaping shadows. Then the shadows came together into a single gigantic figure—a man looming spread-legged at the top of the stairs.

Uncle Ralph stopped. "Who—who's there?" he shouted.

The figure stood, unmoving. The wind roared down at them, and Uncle Ralph seemed to be having trouble holding the flashlight steady.

"Look!" Chris screamed. "Uncle Ralph, look! *The light shines right through him!*"

She let go of the railing, and the wind lifted her and flung her down the steps into the hall. Uncle Ralph was right behind her. They landed in a tangled heap on the floor.

"Close the door!" Chris cried. "Oh, close the door! Quick!" She could hear the thud of descending footsteps.

Uncle Ralph staggered to his feet. He put his shoulder to the door and pushed against the wind with all his strength. The door swung shut with a bang. In the same instant, the raging wind was silenced.

Uncle Ralph leaned against the door, panting. Then he grabbed Chris's hand and pulled her down the hall to his bedroom. Together, they pushed and shoved his heavy oak bureau out into the hall and up against the attic door.

"I'll say this much, Christina," Uncle Ralph gasped as they stepped back from their barricade. "I am now definitely a believer. Your ghost is my ghost."

Chris didn't even think of saying I-told-you-so. It was enough that Uncle Ralph believed her. He wouldn't accuse her again of not knowing the difference between pretending and the truth.

"What'll we do now?" she asked. "Can we go away somewhere? I'm really scared, Uncle Ralph."

"So am I," Uncle Ralph replied. He gave the bureau

another shove to be sure it rested snugly against the door, and then he waved Chris toward the stairs. "We'll talk about it," he said. "In the kitchen. What I need right now is that cup of cocoa."

13.

"Something Very Strange Here"

"Wipe your upper lip, Christina," Uncle Ralph said. "You have a cocoa mustache that's as big as my real one." He was beginning to look and sound more like himself.

Chris rubbed her mouth with the back of her hand. The hot cocoa was warming her insides, and the goose bumps were fading from her arms. Uncle Ralph scowled at the weak overhead light, then brought a kerosene lamp from the cupboard. Its gentle glow made the kitchen almost cheerful.

"That's better," he said. "A little soothing lamplight while we decide what to do next."

"Get out," Chris suggested. "Let's go to Grandma's house and stay there."

Uncle Ralph shook his head. "It isn't that simple," he said. "My friend in Europe is counting on me to stay through the summer. If I leave, I'll have to give him a reasonable explanation. . . . Besides," he hurried on, "we're mixed up in something very strange here. Something very rare. We have to deal with it, not run away."

"Deal with it how?" If he said he was going back up to the attic, Chris was going to leave by herself.

"You told me your ideas of what's happening here," Uncle Ralph said. "And I guess I have to agree with you. As of now. The child—the ghost—we saw in the study is a sad little thing. But that . . . that *presence* in the attic is something else. Dixon, or whatever his name was, must be laid to rest."

"Laid to rest?" Chris didn't like this conversation one bit. Laying Dixon to rest sounded like killing him— but wasn't Dixon already dead?

"The fellow clearly wants something. Or else he wants to keep us away from something. I haven't read a ghost story in forty years, but it seems to me those are the usual reasons given for a ghost to walk. I wonder if it could be those stamps you told me about. You said the police looked for them but couldn't find them. Maybe they're still somewhere in this house. That would explain why Dixon is prowling around. He's keeping his eye on the treasure he died to protect."

Chris shivered. "So what should we do?" she asked. "Hunt for the stamps?"

Uncle Ralph looked at her with approval. "Exactly right, sport," he said. "Starting tomorrow, we'll go over the entire house. We'll save the attic for last," he added hastily, seeing Chris's expression. "If we can find the stamps and turn them over to the police, there won't be any reason for Dixon to stay around. We'll have some peace, and I can get back to my work. What do you say?"

"Okay," Chris said. "I guess." She wondered how he could expect to find anything as small as a stamp in this huge house, but she was willing to try. It would be nice to do something *with* somebody instead of being by herself all day.

They finished their cocoa and rinsed the cups, and Uncle Ralph turned out the lights. Together they trudged to the front hall and looked up the stairs.

"I don't know," Uncle Ralph said after a minute. "Are you going to be able to sleep up there?"

"I don't think so." Chris's goose bumps were coming back.

Uncle Ralph ran his fingers through his hair. "Then how about sleeping down here in the parlor tonight? Both of us." He sounded as if he hoped she'd say yes.

"Terrific!" Chris said. He really could read her mind.

She used the little bathroom under the stairs and then

curled up on the old couch in the parlor. Uncle Ralph
settled in the big chair close to the door.

It was amazing how much better she felt, just knowing he was there. *He's not very big, and I guess he's
as frightened as I am,* she thought, *but he's brave. He
opened that attic door and started up the stairs, when
all I wanted to do was run!*

She didn't think her own father could have been any
braver.

14.

A Warning from Russell Charles

"We'll start our search in the study," Uncle Ralph announced at breakfast. "I'm sure the police did a pretty thorough search at the time of the murders. But there's a good chance they didn't open every single book. That's what we'll do." He sounded excited at the idea.

"Okay." Chris moved her shoulders in circles, trying to loosen the knots. The couch had made a bumpy bed.

She was surprised that Uncle Ralph could sound so full of energy. Twice during the night, she'd opened her eyes to see him leaning forward in his chair, listening intently. Each time she'd held her breath, wondering what he'd heard. When he leaned back and closed his eyes, she'd had to force herself to close her eyes, too. Her dreams had been full of dark, towering figures and footsteps thumping down distant halls.

"You *like* mysteries!" she exclaimed suddenly. "You like ghost hunting, Uncle Ralph."

"Nonsense," Uncle Ralph said. "Things just look different in the daylight. I want to get this business cleared up so I can get back to work." He whistled under his breath while they washed the dishes.

It was strange, Chris thought. They seemed to have exchanged places. She'd been badly frightened the first time she'd opened the attic door, and again the night she'd heard footsteps in the upstairs hall. Still, she hadn't wanted to run away; she'd wanted to solve the mystery. But that was before she'd seen the spirit of Thomas Dixon. Now she couldn't stop thinking about that huge, threatening figure at the top of the attic stairs. She wanted to leave, but Uncle Ralph wanted to solve the mystery, no matter what they had to do.

The study bookshelves, stretching all the way to the ceiling, made her sigh. She was glad the day was dull and drizzly. She didn't think she could have stood it if the weather had been perfect for swimming or a walk in the woods.

"Hold each book like this," Uncle Ralph showed her. "Flip the pages, but don't strain the binding."

By noon, Chris's arms ached and her head throbbed. They had searched through all the books on one wall and had checked the back of each shelf to see if anything was hidden there. Books stood in wobbly piles all around them.

By four o'clock, the second wall had been emptied. "Let's quit," Chris begged. "Otherwise, I'm going to hate books forever."

"If you say so." Uncle Ralph slid one more book back onto its shelf. He looked as if he, too, was beginning to lose hope.

They went out to the kitchen and opened the cupboard.

"Spaghetti?" Uncle Ralph suggested. He pushed the cans around. "Vegetable soup? Hash? Chili?"

They settled, without much enthusiasm, on the roast beef hash. Uncle Ralph fried it and poached eggs to go on top, while Chris mixed powdered milk and opened a can of peaches.

"Now what happens?" she asked when they sat down. She propped her aching head with one hand while she ate.

"We have a few more shelves to check," Uncle Ralph said. "And a few hundred books to put back in place." He scowled. "You know, I was really sure we were going to find something there. After all, Dixon was a teacher as well as a thief. He probably spent a lot of time in the study, when he wasn't looking after the boy. If he wanted a hiding place for a few stamps, what better place . . . ?" He patted his mustache with a paper-towel napkin. "We may still find them," he said.

"But not tonight," Chris protested. "I can't look any more tonight."

Uncle Ralph grinned. "Not tonight," he agreed. "I'm going to settle down in the parlor with a good book." He chuckled at Chris's pained expression. "Reading books is more enjoyable than flipping their pages," he told her. "You ought to try it sometime, sport."

Chris wrinkled her nose at him. "Not tonight," she repeated. "You go ahead and read if you want to. I'll wash the dishes."

Alone in the kitchen, she found herself peeking over her shoulder frequently and jumping at every sound. All day she'd felt as if someone were watching them search through the books. She suspected Uncle Ralph had felt that way, too; he'd stopped often and stood very still, as if he were listening.

What could she do this evening while Uncle Ralph read? She wouldn't mind reading some comic books— they didn't count as real books—but they were in Russell's room upstairs. And she certainly wasn't going up there to get one. She hadn't been upstairs all day, except for a fast early-morning trip, with Uncle Ralph at her side, to get clean underwear, her toothbrush, and a comb.

There was one comic book downstairs, she remembered—the one she'd picked up the first day after they arrived. She'd seen it somewhere, perhaps on the dining-room sideboard. She gave the sink a final wipe and went down the hall. But the sideboard was bare, except for a huge enameled bowl.

For a moment Chris stood there, wondering what else she could do this evening. Then she bent down and looked underneath the sideboard. The comic book was there, behind one of the heavy wooden legs and curled up against the molding.

She carried the book to the parlor. She'd read all the riddles that first day, but she could try them on Uncle Ralph. If she made him laugh, maybe Russell Charles would appear again. And maybe not. It hadn't been the friendly gaze of a little boy that she'd felt while they searched the study.

"Uncle Ralph, why is a mouse like hay?"

He looked up. "You tell me." He sounded impatient.

"Because the cat'll eat it." Chris waited. "See, 'cat'll' sounds the same as 'cattle'—"

"I've told you a hundred times," Uncle Ralph said. "Don't explain."

"What did one candle say to the other candle?"

Uncle Ralph gave up. He closed his book on one finger and pretended to concentrate. "You light up my world?"

Chris giggled. "That's pretty good," she admitted. "But it's the wrong answer. The right answer is 'Are you going out tonight?'"

Uncle Ralph shrugged. "I like mine better. Or how about 'I think you're really *wick*-ed, dearie'?"

It was Chris's turn to groan. She read him the last riddle on the page. "What goes 'Ho-ho-ho-thunk'?"

"I've heard that one before," Uncle Ralph said, but now the playfulness was gone from his voice. "It's a man laughing his head off."

Chris looked up from the comic book. Uncle Ralph was staring at a corner of the parlor. There was the slightest of movements, and suddenly Russell Charles was standing there.

"He came back," Chris breathed. "Oh, I'm glad."

But this time Russell wasn't smiling. The small face seemed frozen in panic. As Chris and Uncle Ralph watched, he raised a hand and pointed at Chris. Then, as silently as he'd come, he was gone.

"Something's wrong," Chris cried. "He never looked like that before. Oh, Uncle Ralph—"

She stopped as a loud scraping sound cut through the quiet house. It came from upstairs.

"The chest," Uncle Ralph said. Beads of sweat popped out on his forehead. "That was the chest being pushed away from the attic door."

"No," Chris whimpered. "No, no, no!"

But even as she said it, she heard the attic door open, and heavy steps started down the upstairs hall.

15.

"Let's Get Out of Here!"

Uncle Ralph crossed the parlor in one long leap. He snatched the comic book from Chris's hands and flipped the pages.

"He's coming!" Chris shrieked. "Listen!"

The footsteps reached the top of the stairs. "He's going to come down," Chris said. "Let's get out of here!"

"And do you know *why* he's coming down?" Uncle Ralph demanded hoarsely. "We're getting too close to his secret, that's why. Russell Charles was trying to tell us something." He shook the comic book hard. A glassine envelope, long and narrow like a bookmark, fell to the floor.

"There it is!" he shouted.

The footsteps started down the stairs.

Uncle Ralph dived for the envelope, but before he could pick it up, an icy wind swept the room. The envelope skittered across the carpet.

"I'll get it," Chris squealed. She snatched up the envelope and looked around for an escape route. Not the front door. That would mean facing the thing that was on the stairs. She ran to a window. The nearest one was painted shut. She struggled with the second until Uncle Ralph pushed her aside and jerked it open.

"Out you go!" he shouted. "Quick!"

The cold wind roared around Chris, and the footsteps on the stairs were as loud as thunder. She tumbled through the window out onto the porch. Uncle Ralph was right behind her. At the top of the steps he grabbed her hand, and they jumped off the porch together.

"Around the back," Uncle Ralph panted. "Head for the car."

Chris felt as if she were running through a swamp that sucked at her feet and held her back. "Can't— can't run!" she gasped.

Uncle Ralph pulled her along. "Yes you can," he said. "Just make sure you hang on to that envelope, sport."

They reached the car. Uncle Ralph swung open the

door on the driver's side and threw Chris across
the seat. Then he jumped in after her and slammed the
door. The keys were in the ignition. There was a heart-
stopping moment when the motor stuttered, quit, then
roared to life.

"That's my good old baby," Uncle Ralph muttered.
"That's my girl!"

He swung the car around so that the headlights rested
full on the house. Curtains and draperies billowed furiously at every window. Lights flicked on and off, all
over the house. Then the back door flew open, and the
towering figure of the attic ghost was silhouetted in
the headlights' beam.

"He's coming!" Chris screamed. "He's coming after
us!"

Uncle Ralph pulled hard on the wheel, and the car
shot into the narrow, winding road that led to the highway. The trees formed a tunnel around them, and as
the car bounced through it, the branches ahead seemed
to bend down. Something struck the roof a sharp blow.

"He's trying to stop us," Chris cried. "What are we
going to do?"

Uncle Ralph clutched the steering wheel like a race-
car driver. "Hang on, sport," he said through clenched
teeth. "This is still Dixon's territory. Do you have that
envelope?"

Chris held up the strip of glassine.

"Good. Don't wrinkle it."

"Wrinkle it!" Chris exclaimed. "I can hardly hold it, I'm shaking so hard."

"Then put it in the glove compartment, and go ahead and shake," Uncle Ralph snapped. He winced as a branch scraped across the windshield. "We're almost back to civilization."

As he said it, they shot out onto the highway. A semitrailer truck swerved around them with startled blasts of the horn.

"Cool it, bub," Uncle Ralph said. He raced after the truck. Other cars were coming toward them now, their lights reassuring in the forest dark. Far ahead, the lights of a woodland motel twinkled.

"We're okay!" Uncle Ralph said. "We've made it!" But Chris noticed that he didn't slow down. Not until the gas stations, bait shops, and small shingled houses of Clearwater began flying past did he take his foot off the gas.

"There's a little coffee shop right smack in the middle of town," he said. "We'll go there."

Good, Chris thought. Ghosts didn't show themselves in coffee shops, did they?

When they parked in front of the little restaurant, Chris discovered that her knees were still trembling. She shook as she removed the envelope from the glove compartment, followed Uncle Ralph into the restaurant and settled in a high-backed booth. She laid the glassine envelope in the middle of the table and stared at it.

Across from her, Uncle Ralph wiped his face with his handkerchief. He took deep breaths, like a swimmer coming up for air. "You want to open that thing, Christina?" he asked. "You deserve to. You're the one who got it away from—from *him.*"

Chris shuddered. She glanced out at the street, where tourists strolled, eating ice-cream cones and enjoying the soft summer night. She would have liked to be one of them. Walking down Clearwater's main street eating an ice-cream cone was all the adventure she'd ever want again.

"We'll do that tomorrow," Uncle Ralph said, once again seeming to read her mind. "Open that envelope, will you?"

Chris worked a grubby fingernail under the envelope's flap. Two strips of stamps slipped out on the table. There were four silver-gray ones with a picture of George Washington. The other strip was made up of five stamps printed in reddish-brown.

"Who's that?" Chris asked.

Uncle Ralph stared at the stamps in awe. "That's Benjamin Franklin," he said. He touched the strips with a cautious finger. "I don't know much about stamps," he said slowly, "but I've seen pictures of both of these. And I've read about them. They're part of the very first stamp-issue printed by the United States Government."

"The very first?" And she'd carried them around in a comic book! "They don't have those little holes to help you tear them apart," she pointed out. "Maybe they're fakes."

Uncle Ralph shook his head. "In 1847, when these were printed, the government didn't use perforations. That came later. The fact that these are in such perfect condition and haven't been cut apart makes them especially valuable, I'm sure."

Chris was thrilled. She thought of the millions of stamps on millions of letters on their way to people all over the country. Finding these first ones was like . . . like uncovering a national treasure.

The waitress brought Uncle Ralph coffee and the cinnamon-apple pie he'd ordered. Chris had a chocolate milkshake and a cheese sandwich. She discovered she was starving, and Uncle Ralph seemed just as hungry. They ate without talking, but Chris realized that this silence was nothing like the gloomy silence of their first meals together.

A couple of times, Uncle Ralph patted the pocket where he'd put the stamps for safekeeping. When the pie was gone and his cup had been filled for the second time, he leaned back with a sigh.

"Now let's take another look," he said. He laid the

stamps on the table again. "Do you realize how close
we came to missing these?" he said. "If you weren't
a comic-book fan, for example. . . ."

"And if I hadn't left the right book in the dining
room," Chris said. She was remembering an afternoon
when she'd taken a couple of the comics out to the end
of the pier. One of them had blown into the water while
she sunbathed.

"And if it weren't for Russell Charles," Uncle Ralph
added. "Poor little kid—caught up in a mystery he
didn't want any part of."

"I wonder what he'll do now," Chris said. "And
what's going to happen to that awful Dixon? Do you
think he's going to go thumping and raging around the
house forever and ever?"

Uncle Ralph slid the stamps back into their envelope.
"All I'm sure of," he said, "is that we're not going
back tonight to find out." Then he leaned across the
table and raised an eyebrow at Chris. "Unless, of course,
you insist on it, Christina. I'll go if you want to. We
aim to please."

16.

Two of a Kind

They checked and found that the only motel on Clear-water's main street was filled with tourists.

"We could go back to that motel we passed on the highway," Uncle Ralph said. "Or we can sleep in the car. What do you think?"

"The car," Chris said at once. She didn't want to leave the lights of town.

Uncle Ralph looked relieved. "The car it is," he said. "This is going to be a short night, anyway."

He parked just off the main street, and after making sure Chris was comfortable in back, he settled down in the driver's seat. His shock of grey hair, silvered by the street light, was the last thing Chris saw before she slept. *Good old Uncle Ralph,* she thought. He understood how she felt about staying in Clearwater tonight. He felt the same way.

They woke early when a little boy tapped on the windshield and grinned at them. Uncle Ralph drove to the sheriff's office.

"I'll be glad to get rid of these," he said, touching the pocket that held the stamps. "I've never been in charge of a fortune before."

Chris waited in the car and almost fell asleep again before he returned, looking pleased with himself.

"The sheriff was pretty surprised," he told Chris as they headed back to the coffee shop for breakfast. "It isn't every day that evidence turns up to explain a thirty-year-old crime."

"Did you tell him about the ghosts?"

"Now, that's a silly question," Uncle Ralph said. "I told him we found some valuable stamps. In a comic book. Accidentally. I did *not* tell them about Russell Charles or about Thomas Dixon, or about cold winds blowing through the house or footsteps going *thunk* in the night. I have my reputation to think of, you know."

"But it did happen," Chris said, a little doubtfully. In the bright light of morning, with good smells of breakfast toast and bacon around them, last night's adventure was beginning to seem unreal.

"It did happen," Uncle Ralph assured her. "You know it, and I know it. But there's no reason why anyone else has to hear about it. Agreed?"

"Except Mom and Dad," Chris said.

"If you must."

They left it at that. An hour later, they were on their way back to the house, and Chris was struggling to ignore a whole flock of butterflies in her stomach. *Not butterflies,* she thought. *Eagles!*

"We have to go back at least once, sport," Uncle Ralph had insisted. "Or at least I do. My notes are there and my typewriter—to say nothing of our clothes. You can wait in town if you'd rather."

"Oh, no!" It wouldn't be fair to make him go back to that house alone.

"Good girl," Uncle Ralph said. "If there's anything strange going on, we'll just grab our stuff and get out. Permanently."

"Right," Chris had agreed. Now she held her breath as the car made its final turn into the yard behind the house.

A blue sedan was parked near the back steps. As Chris and Uncle Ralph stared at it in astonishment, Aunt Grace climbed out on one side and Jenny on the other.

"Good grief!" Uncle Ralph groaned. "Not now!"

But Aunt Grace was waving a greeting, and Jenny came flying across the grass to meet them, her blond hair shining in the sun.

"Where were you?" she shouted. "Grandma's coming home today, Chrissy. We're going to get her."

"Hi, Jenny." Chris gave her little sister a hug, but her eyes were on the house. All the windows were open. The curtains hung straight and still.

"Where in the world have you two been?" Aunt Grace demanded. "Going off and leaving this place open to anyone who wandered by. Really, Ralph!"

"We had to go to town," Uncle Ralph said. "And no one wanders by here—except you, Grace." He scowled. "You didn't go in, did you?"

"Of course I didn't go in," Aunt Grace snapped. "I don't walk uninvited into other people's houses. I wasn't even sure this was the right place. But the car was gone, and I thought surely if it *was* the right place, you'd be back soon. I mean, with all the windows open and the door open. . . ." Her voice trailed off as Uncle Ralph marched past her up the steps and disappeared inside the house.

For just one moment, Chris hesitated. She felt so safe out here with Aunt Grace and Jenny. Birds sang in the woods, and the air buzzed with insects. Then she ran up the steps after Uncle Ralph.

"Well, honestly," Aunt Grace said, and followed with Jenny.

The kitchen was warm and full of light. The worn brick floor gave back a ruddy glow, and the white-painted cabinets shone in the sun.

"Why, this is really quite nice," Aunt Grace said, sounding surprised. "These old houses can be so damp and musty."

That was what was different, Chris thought. The musty smell was gone, and the gloom had gone with it.

They followed Uncle Ralph as he led the way down the hall, into the parlor, through the dining room and study, and back to the front hall. Aunt Grace and Jenny thought they were being given a tour, but Chris knew Uncle Ralph wanted to look around. Except for the books piled on the floor of the study, there was no trace of the terrifying events of the night before. The rooms were bright and still.

"Christina, you take Jenny upstairs and show her your bedroom," Aunt Grace ordered. "I want to talk to Ralph for a while. We have to make plans now that your grandmother's coming home."

Chris looked at Uncle Ralph, wide-eyed. *Upstairs?*

"You don't have to," Uncle Ralph said quickly. "We can all go up and look around later."

Chris gulped. "That's okay," she said. "I think everything's all right now."

"So do I," Uncle Ralph replied. "Or I wouldn't let you go."

Aunt Grace frowned. "What in the world—"

"Come on, Grace," Uncle Ralph said. "I'll make coffee. Tell me about Ma."

Jenny crowded close to Chris as they climbed the stairs. "It's awful at Aunt Grace's," she whispered. "I have to eat liver and peas. And she *boils* the chicken. And I can't watch any good television shows." She poked Chris in the ribs. "I bet it was awful staying with Uncle Ralph, too."

They had reached the top of the stairs. All the doors except that of Chris's bedroom were closed. The chest was against the wall at the end of the corridor. And the air was fresh and sweet, with a lake breeze blowing through Chris's bedroom window.

"It wasn't so bad here," said Chris.

Jenny peeked briefly into Chris's room and then turned to the door next to it. "What's in here?" she demanded, and threw the door open. "Hey, it's a little kid's room! Oh, I wish I'd stayed here instead of with Aunt Grace. This would have been my room for sure." She darted around, admiring the posters and running her fingers over the game boxes on the shelves.

Chris stood in the doorway. The room had changed.

"Even the bed is my size," Jenny squealed. "Look!"

Chris looked. The bed covers, which had been turned back and waiting for thirty years, were pulled up and neatly smoothed.

She crossed the red carpet and stood beside Jenny. *Good-bye, Russell,* she thought. She touched the pillow, knowing, as surely as if he'd told her, that she wouldn't see the little boy again. He could rest peacefully now that the stamps were found and the last mystery surrounding his death was solved.

"Come on," Jenny shouted. "I want to see the rest of the rooms."

She ran away and down the hall, throwing open bedroom doors left and right. "If I stayed here, I'd sleep in a different room every night," she announced. "You picked the worst room, silly old Chrissy. . . . What's in here?"

Her hand was on the attic door.

"Nothing," Chris cried. "Don't open it!"

Jenny paid no attention. She had the door open and was partway up the stairs when Chris reached her.

"Big deal," she said, shaking off Chris's hand. "This is nothing but a stuffy old attic. Boring."

The staircase was warm and dusty. Chris forced herself to look up, where the dust floated in bright beams of sunlight. "Boring," she agreed. She leaned against the wall until she stopped shaking.

When they went downstairs, Uncle Ralph and Aunt Grace were in the kitchen drinking coffee with a box of gingersnaps between them. Uncle Ralph looked at Chris and raised his eyebrows. She shook her head, and he leaned back with a satisfied nod.

"Ralph tells me you're welcome to stay on here if you wish, Christina." Aunt Grace watched her suspiciously. "I plan to run out to the farm every day for a while to see how your grandmother's doing, so I suppose you don't have to come back with us today to help. It's up to you."

Chris thought about what it would be like at the farm. She could talk for hours with Grandma and play games with Jenny. She could go exploring with Maggie the sheepdog and fish in the stream. The long, lonely days would be ended.

Uncle Ralph smiled at her. "And besides all that," he said, reading her mind once again, "you wouldn't have to eat canned hash and canned chili every day."

Chris felt her face turn red. "I don't care about that," she said fiercely. "I like being with you, Uncle Ralph."

They stared at each other, and Chris smiled, too. The words had astonished them both.

"But I guess I'll go to Grandma's," she said. "There's stuff I can do."

Uncle Ralph nodded. "Don't blame you a bit," he said. "I'll miss you, but I have my work and I want to stick with it. You and I are two of a kind, sport—independent as they come."

Jenny leaned across the table, eager to be part of the conversation. "Chris is a tomboy," she protested. "She always gets into trouble. You don't like tomboys."

"Times change," Uncle Ralph said. He helped himself to another gingersnap. "So do uncles." He winked at Chris, who winked back.

Betty Ren Wright

When she was eight, Betty Ren Wright began copying her poems into a loose-leaf notebook with her name lettered across the cover. That was her first book, and she liked the idea so much she never stopped writing. She attended grade school, high school, and college in the Milwaukee, Wisconsin, area, and took every opportunity to write. Her first short story, a mystery, was published soon after graduation, and her first picture book appeared a couple of years later.

For many years, Betty Ren was an editor of children's books and did most of her writing in her spare time. In 1976 she married and became step-grandmother to a large family. Two years later she left editing to write full-time. She is the author of the successful novel *The Dollhouse Murders,* the recipient of nine state awards, among many others. She lives near Kenosha, Wisconsin.

Exclusive Author Interview with . . .
BETTY REN WRIGHT

What types of books did you like to read when you were a child?

I read constantly, and pretty indiscriminately; my mother brought home armfuls of books from the Teachers College library every Friday, and I swallowed them whole. I loved family stories, animal stories (no matter how sentimental!). I did not care for fantasy; I craved ghost stories, but I wanted the ghosts to appear to ordinary people like me.

That's why you write ghost stories!

I've always loved ghost stories; but when I was growing up, there always had to be an explanation for what appeared supernatural. I wanted *real* ghosts, and starting with *The Dollhouse Murders*, I found them. I'm so glad there were lots of readers who wanted the same thing.

Where do the ideas for your books come from?

Well, like most writers I use my own experiences and the experiences of friends as starting points. Or I remember feelings I had in childhood and start there. Each time, the finished story is very different from what actually happened, because as I start writing I constantly ask myself, 'What if . . .? What if that dollhouse were haunted? What if I were ten years old and had to spend the whole summer with a bachelor uncle who didn't like children? What if my dreams actually came true, and I was afraid to tell my family what was happening?' I consider lots of different what-ifs for each book; and by the time I've chosen my favorites, the book has begun to take shape.

Tell us about two of your most popular books, *The Dollhouse Murders* **and** *Christina's Ghost.*

The Dollhouse Murders really began the day I watched two young brothers, one of them mentally challenged, sharing a picnic at a roadside stop. The direction of the novel was settled the day I helped my friend "clean" her dollhouse (we used very delicate watercolor brushes).

The setting for *Christina's Ghost* grew out of the many hours I spent as a child at an isolated lake cottage. When I was a little girl, my mother periodically decided I should experience "family life"; and off I went to stay with an aunt, uncle, and four teenage cousins. I never forgot the feelings of total dislocation that went with those visits—my aunt was accustomed to four teenage boys, and the boys barely noticed the visitor curled up in the library with a book. I wanted to reproduce some of the lost feeling in Christina's summer with Uncle Ralph, but I wanted Christina to be as unlike me as possible. She acknowledged her discomfort, but unlike me she set out to do something about it. She became the girl I wished I had been.

Do you have a favorite spooky, old house that you visited or ever stayed in?

For a dozen years or so I lived in an apartment created from the sunroom of a huge hundred-year-old house in Racine. It was sometimes drafty but always sunny, and it had a fine working fireplace. I loved every minute of my time there, even after the owners, who lived in the rest of the house, told me it was haunted. Unfortunately the ghost or ghosts never visited the sunroom.

What were your favorite books growing up?

I like the old-fashioned stories (old-fashioned even when I was a child) such as *Little Women*, *Little Men*, *Treasure Island*, and *Black*

Beauty. In my grandparents' little library I discovered a treasure trove of Horatio Alger (my uncle's), and I read some Nancy Drew, though she wasn't a great favorite. Later, *Precious Bane* by Mary Webb became my "best book ever"—a kind of real-life fairy tale.

What have you learned about yourself through your writing?

Writing for young people has made me look back and examine my childhood and the influences that formed me. I guess I've learned to look back without blinking.

What advice do you have for young writers?

I have one answer: Read, read, READ! Read both fiction and nonfiction. That's probably the most important! Make use of every opportunity to write, even if it's an assignment that doesn't particularly interest you. Read the works of many writers and ask yourself which you like the best and why. Try to decide what your favorite authors have done to make their books interesting. You'll develop taste and judgment that will help you to do your best work when you sit down to write.

Happy reading !
Betty Ren Wright